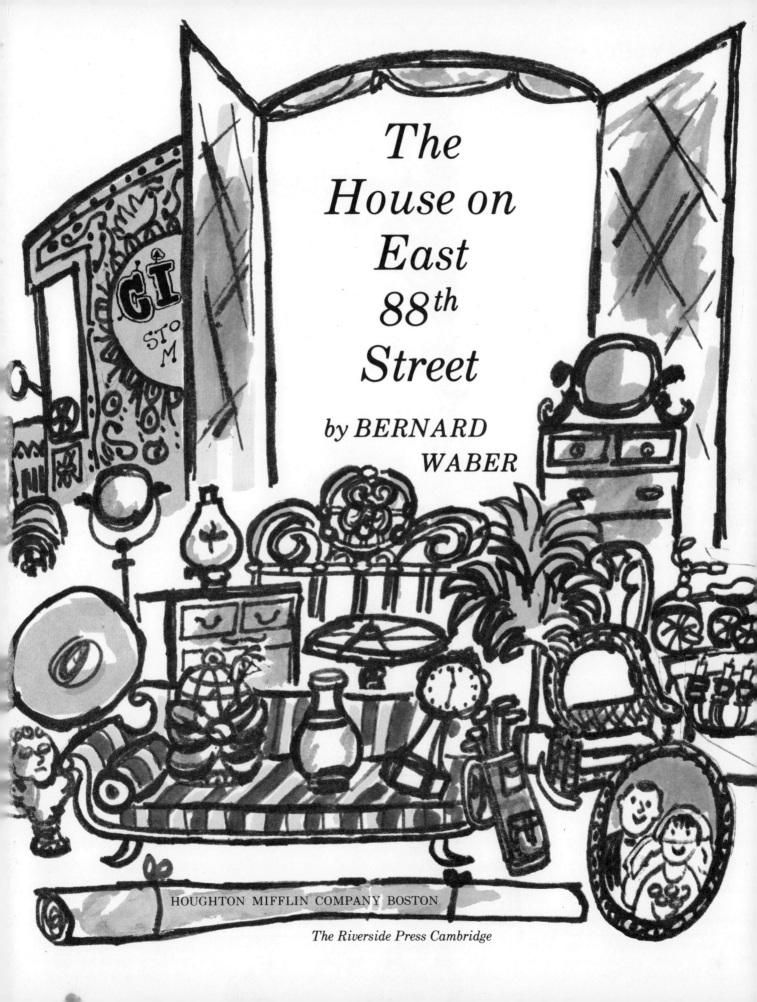

The House on East 88th Street

by BERNARD WABER

HOUGHTON MIFFLIN COMPANY BOSTON

The Riverside Press Cambridge

for *Paulis*

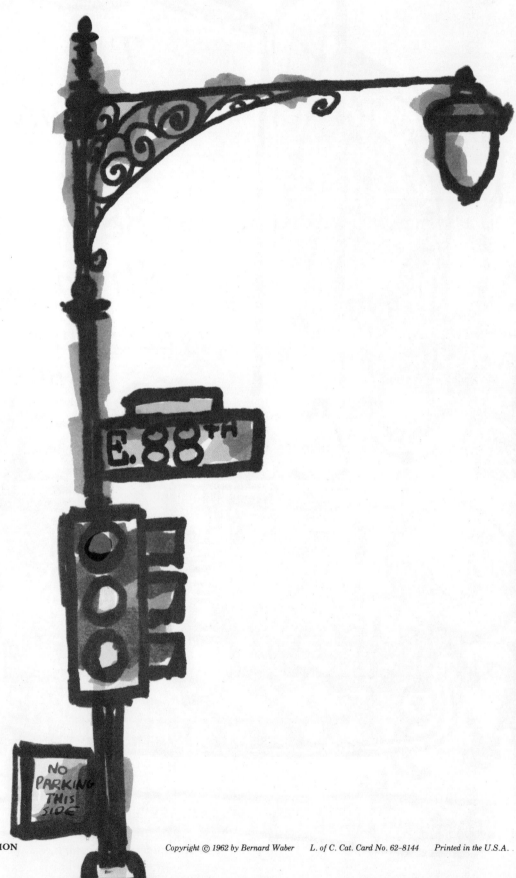

WEEKLY READER BOOK CLUB EDITION   *Copyright © 1962 by Bernard Waber   L. of C. Cat. Card No. 62-8144   Printed in the U.S.A.*

This is the house.
The house on
East 88th Street.
It is empty now,
but it won't be
for long.
Strange sounds come
from the house.
Can you hear them?
Listen:
SWISH, SWASH,
SPLASH, SWOOSH . . .

It began one sunny morning
when the Citywide Storage
and Moving Company truck
pulled up to the house on
East 88th Street and unloaded
the belongings of
Mr. and Mrs. Joseph F. Primm
and their young son Joshua.

It was a trying day for everyone. Mrs. Primm just couldn't decide where to put the piano. And Mr. Primm's favorite pipe was accidentally packed away in one of dozens of cartons lying about.

SWISH, SWASH, SPLASH, SWOOSH.
Loudly and clearly the sounds
now rumbled through the house.
"It's only a little thunder,"
Mrs. Primm assured everyone.
When a Citywide Storage and
Moving man carried in their
potted pistachio tree, everyone
rejoiced; the truck was at
last empty. The movers wished
them well and hurried off to
their next job for the day.

"Now I'm going to prepare our lunch,"
announced Mrs. Primm. "But first I want
to go upstairs and wash these grimy hands."
SWISH, SWASH, SPLASH, SWOOSH . . .
A puzzled Mrs. Primm stopped to listen.
By and by her ears directed her
to the bathroom door.
"What can it be?" she asked herself
as she opened the door.

What she saw made her slam it quickly shut.

Mrs. Primm knew she was going to scream and just
waited for it to happen. But she couldn't scream.
She could scarcely even talk. The most Mrs. Primm
was able to manage was the sharp hoarse whisper of a
voice which she used to call Mr. Primm.
"Joseph," she said, "there's a crocodile
in our bathtub."
Mr. Primm looked into the bathroom.

The next moment found them
flying off in different directions.
"Help, help," Mrs. Primm cried out
as she struggled with a window
stuck with fresh paint.

"Operator, operator," Mr. Primm
shouted into the telephone, and
then he remembered that it was
not yet connected.

Joshua, who had heard everything,
raced to the front door, to be
greeted there by an oddly dressed man who
handed him a note. "This will explain
everything about the crocodile," said
the man, leaving quietly but swiftly.

Mr. Primm read the note:

Please be kind to my crocodile.
He is the most gentle of creatures
and would not do harm to a flea.
He must have tender, loving care,
for he is an artist and can perform
many good tricks. Perhaps he will
perform some for you.

I shall return.

Cordially,

Hector P. Valenti

HECTOR P. VALENTI
Star of stage and screen

P.S. He will eat only Turkish caviar.
P.P.S. His name is Lyle.

"Turkish caviar indeed," exclaimed Mrs. Primm.
"Oh, to think this could happen on East 88th Street.
Whatever will we do with him?"

Suddenly, before anyone could think
of a worthy answer, there was Lyle.

15

And just as suddenly
he got hold of a ball
that had been lying
among Joshua's
belongings and began
to balance it on
his nose . . .
and roll it down the
notches of his spine.

Now he was walking
on his front feet . . .
and taking flying leaps.

17

Now he was twirling Joshua's hoop,
doing it so expertly that the Primms
just had to clap their hands and laugh.
Lyle bowed appreciatively.
He had won his way into their hearts
and into their new home.

"Every home should have a crocodile," said Mrs. Primm one day.
"Lyle is one of the family now. He loves helping out with chores."

"He won't allow anyone else to carry out old newspapers . . . or take in the milk."

"He folds towels,
feeds the bird,
and when he sets the table
there is always a surprise."

"I had only to show him once how to make up a bed."

"People everywhere stop to talk with him.
They say he is the nicest crocodile they ever met."

"Lyle likes to play in the park.
He always goes once around
in the pony cart."

"And now he has learned to eat
something besides Turkish caviar."

"Lyle is a good sport. Everyone wants him to play on his side."

"He is wonderful company. We take him everywhere."

"Just give him his Turkish caviar
and his bed of warm water
and he is happy as a bird."

One day a brass band paraded
past the house on East 88th Street.
The Primm family rushed to the window
to watch. They called for Lyle,
but there was no answer.

"Look," someone pointed out. "It's Lyle, he's in the parade."
There was Lyle doing his specialty of somersault,
flying leaps, walking on front feet and taking bows
just as he did the first day they laid eyes on him.
The people watching cheered him on, while Lyle smiled back at
them and blew kisses. A photographer
was on hand to take pictures.

The next day Lyle was famous.
The telephone rang continually
and bundles of mail were dropped by
the door. One letter was from
someone Lyle knew particularly
well. Mr. Primm read it:

Just a few words to say
I shall return.

                    Cordially,

                    HECTOR P. VALENTI
                    Star of stage and screen

P.S. Very soon.
P.P.S. To fetch my crocodile.

Several days later, Mrs. Primm and Lyle
were in the kitchen shelling peas when
they heard a knocking at the door.
It was Hector P. Valenti, star of stage and screen.
"I have come for Lyle," announced Signor Valenti.

"You can't have Lyle," cried Mrs. Primm,
"he is very happy living here, and we
love him dearly."
"Lyle must be returned to me,"
insisted Signor Valenti.
"Was it not I who raised him from
young crocodilehood?
Was it not I who taught him
his bag of tricks?
We have appeared together on
stages the world over."
"But why then did you leave him
alone in a strange house?" asked Mrs. Primm.
"Because," answered Signor Valenti,
"I could no longer afford to pay for
his Turkish caviar. But now
Lyle is famous and we shall be very rich."
Mrs. Primm was saddened, but she
knew Lyle properly belonged to
Signor Valenti and she had
to let him go.

It was a tearful parting for everyone.

Signor Valenti had
big plans for Lyle.
They were to travel far and wide . . .

stay in many hotels . . .

where sometimes the tubs were too big . . .

and other times too small . . .

or too crowded.

Signor Valenti did what he could
to coax a smile from Lyle.
He tried making funny
faces at him . . .
he stood on his head.

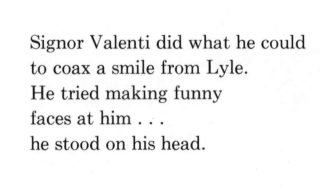

He tickled his toes and told him uproarious stories
that in happier days would have had Lyle doubled over with laughter.
But Lyle could not laugh. Nor could he make people laugh.
He made them cry instead . . . One night in Paris, he made an
entire audience cry. The theater manager was furious
and ordered them off his stage.

Meanwhile at the house on East 88th Street
Mrs. Primm went about her work without her usual bright smile.
And deep sighs could be heard coming
from behind the newspaper Mr. Primm was reading.

Every morning Joshua anxiously awaited the arrival of the mailman in hope of receiving word from Lyle. One morning a letter did come. He knew the handwriting very well.

Just a few words to say
we shall return.

                    Cordially,
                    Hector P. Valenti
                    HECTOR P. VALENTI
                    Former star of stage and screen

P.S. I am sick of crocodiles.
P.P.S. And the tears of crocodiles.

Not too many days after, the Primms
were delighted to find Hector P. Valenti
and Lyle at their door.
"Here, take him back," said Signor Valenti.
"He is no good. He will never make
anyone laugh again."
But Signor Valenti was very much mistaken.
Everyone laughed . . .
and laughed . . . and laughed.
And in the end so did Signor Valenti.

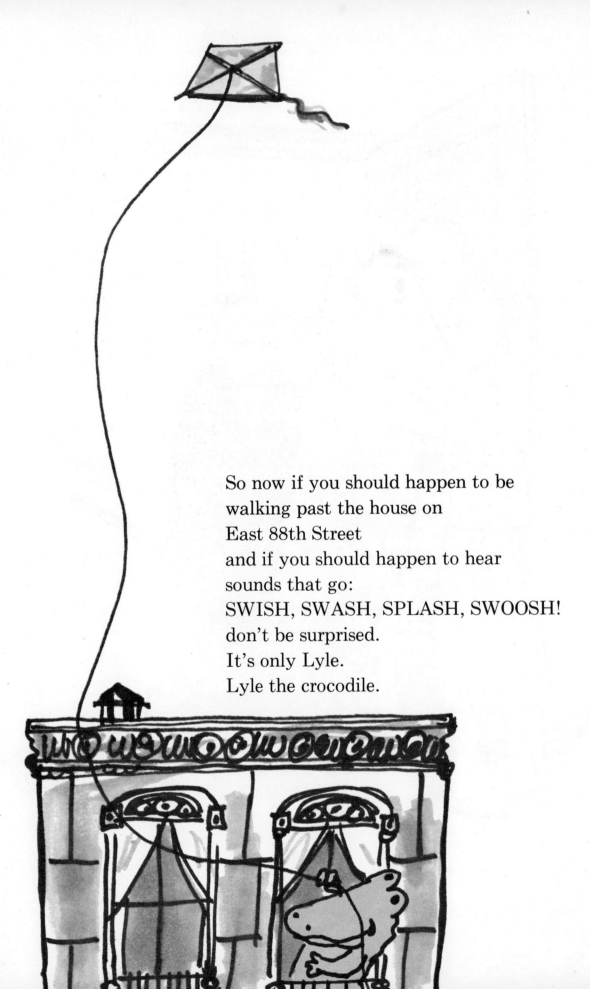

So now if you should happen to be
walking past the house on
East 88th Street
and if you should happen to hear
sounds that go:
SWISH, SWASH, SPLASH, SWOOSH!
don't be surprised.
It's only Lyle.
Lyle the crocodile.